I WANT TO BE A
MUSEUM CURATOR

Written by
Jocelyn Chua

Edited by
Jonathan Reule

Illustration
Caballero Peza Mauricio
&
Caballero Peza Gabriel Fernando

Storyboard
Christiane Tee

UNIBINO
BOOKS

First paperback edition October 2023
ISBN 978-981-17320-3-4

Published by Unibino Pte. Ltd.
9 North Buona Vista Drive, #02-01 Metropolis Tower 1, Singapore 138588

www.unibino.com

Do you ever wonder how the items that you use, such as your toothbrush or pencil, first came about? Do you enjoy collecting things like stuffed toys, stickers, or comic books and creating a unique collection? Do you love sharing with your friends and family about the origins of each of your collected items? If you said yes to any of the above, then you may just have the knack for being a museum curator!

A museum curator is someone who oversees the exhibition of artefacts or collections in a museum. They ensure that these items are well-documented, handled with care, and displayed in both an accurate and engaging manner to those who visit the museum. A curator also manages the acquisition, sale, exchange, and loan of these collections.

But what exactly is a museum, and what is it for? Are there different types of museums, and if so, what are they? Do you know the name of the earliest museum ever discovered in our world? (And can you guess where that museum is currently located?) Let's explore the concept and purpose of a museum in order to better understand what it takes to be a museum curator.

Museums are places that preserve, interpret, and display important historical, cultural, natural, artistic, or scientific objects in ways that can bring us great awareness and understanding of our past. A museum can be privately owned by an individual, group, or organisation. It can also be publicly owned and run by the government.

The earliest known museum is Ennigaldi-Nanna's museum, discovered in what is now recognised as the geographic region of Iraq. Dating back to around 530 BC, the museum was discovered in 1925 by British archaeologist Sir Charles Leonard Woolley. It was built by a Babylonian princess named Ennigaldi - quite possibly the world's first-ever museum curator!

Princess Ennigaldi's museum was dedicated to Mesopotamian artefacts discovered by her father King Nabonidus, the Babylonian king Nebuchadnezzar the Great, and other items by the princess herself. These artefacts were already many centuries old during the princess's time and were used to explain the ancient heritage of her dynasty. The items were found neatly arranged and came with descriptive text written on clay cylinders – the oldest known museum labels!

But did you know that the word 'museum' has its roots in the Greek mouseion, which means 'seat of the Muses' or a place of contemplation? In fact, the early Alexandrian Museum, founded by King Ptolemy I Soter in 300 BC, was initially a place where people could study and express themselves through music and poetry.

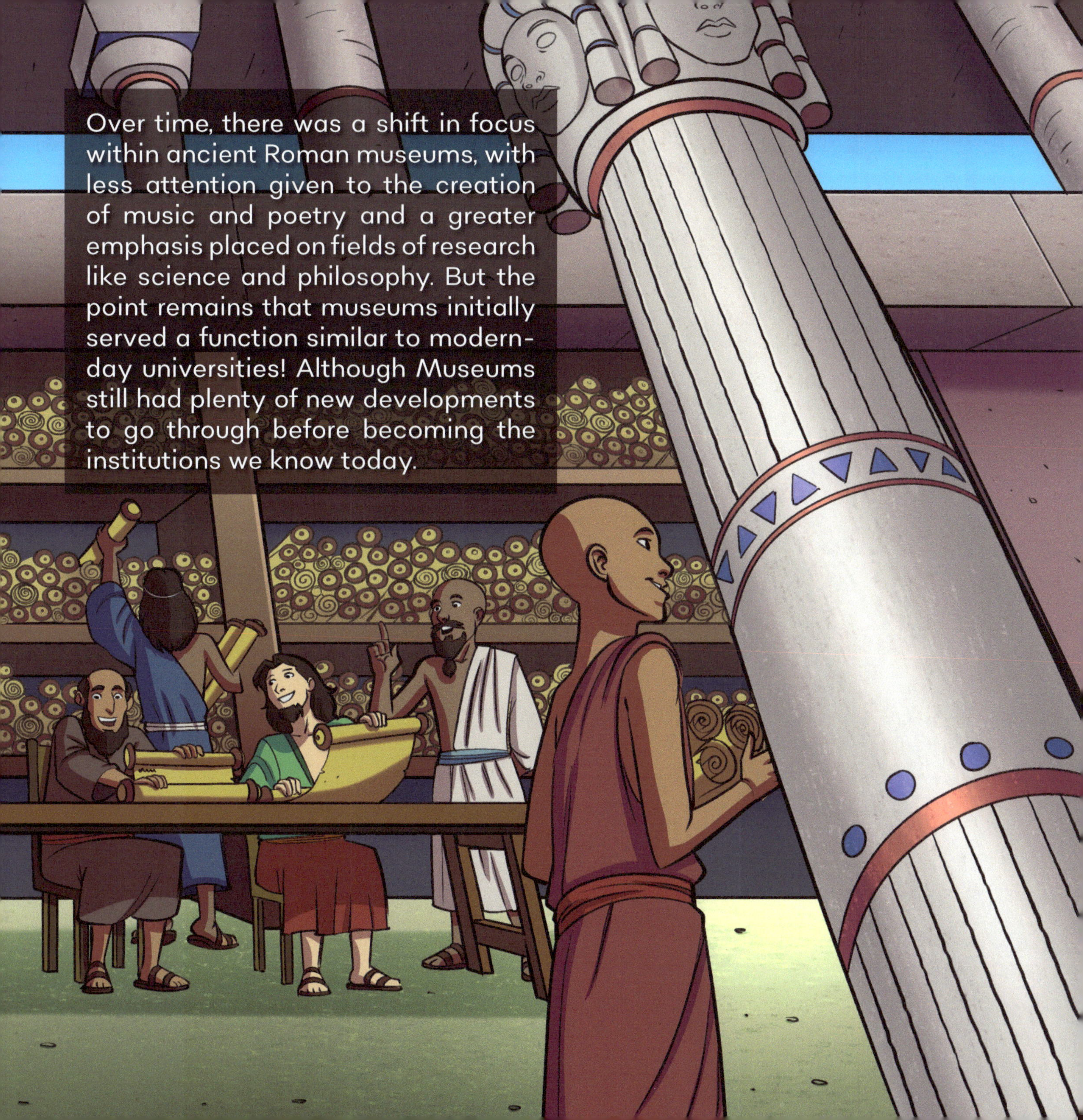
Over time, there was a shift in focus within ancient Roman museums, with less attention given to the creation of music and poetry and a greater emphasis placed on fields of research like science and philosophy. But the point remains that museums initially served a function similar to modern-day universities! Although Museums still had plenty of new developments to go through before becoming the institutions we know today.

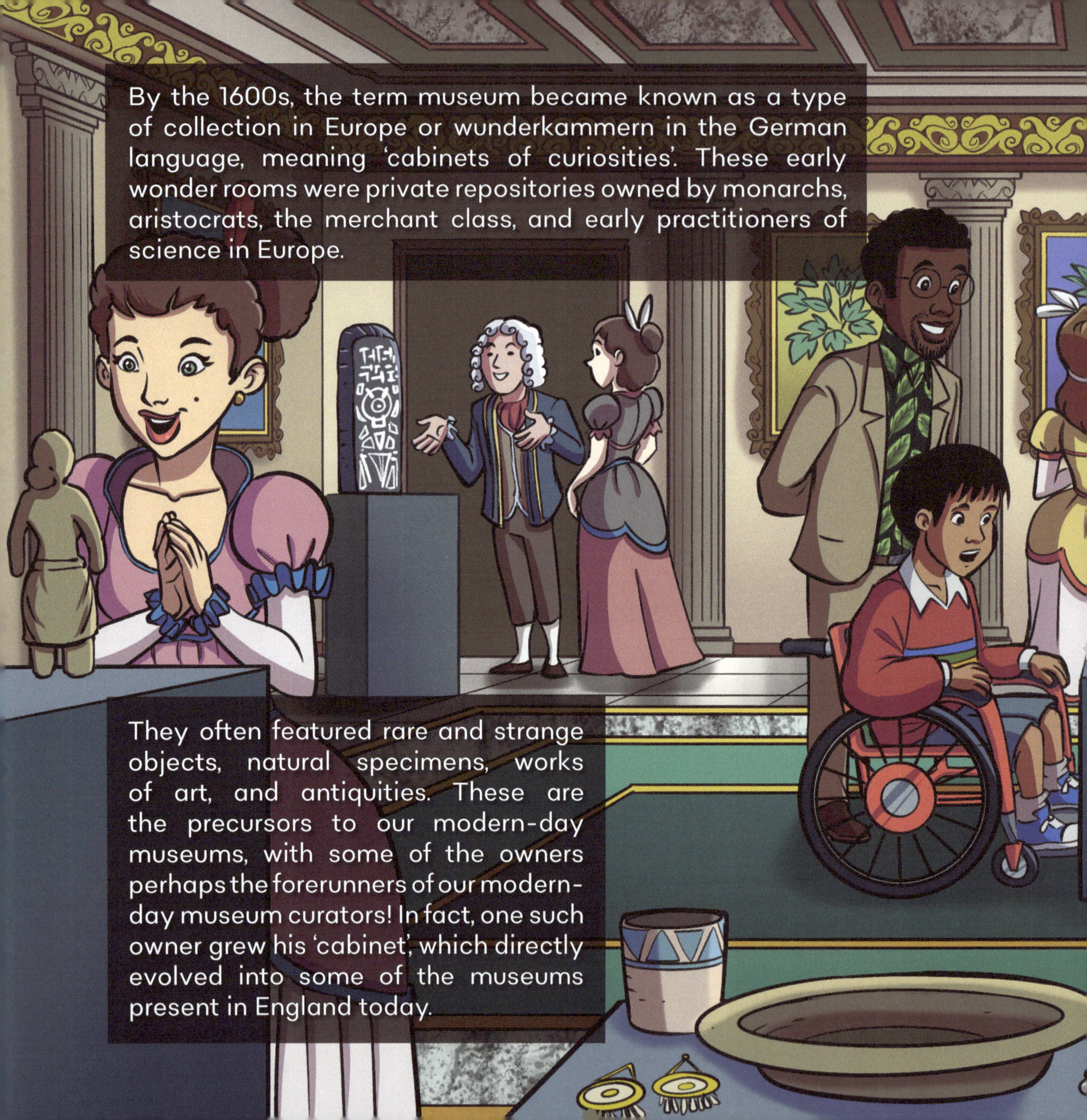

By the 1600s, the term museum became known as a type of collection in Europe or wunderkammern in the German language, meaning 'cabinets of curiosities'. These early wonder rooms were private repositories owned by monarchs, aristocrats, the merchant class, and early practitioners of science in Europe.

They often featured rare and strange objects, natural specimens, works of art, and antiquities. These are the precursors to our modern-day museums, with some of the owners perhaps the forerunners of our modern-day museum curators! In fact, one such owner grew his 'cabinet', which directly evolved into some of the museums present in England today.

Founder of the British Museum in London, Sir Hans Sloane (1660 - 1753), spent fifteen months collecting native plants, animals, and cultural artefacts while working as a physician in Jamaica, returning to England in 1689 with 800 specimens of plants.

Over the decades, Sloane continued to expand and meticulously catalogue his collection, including animal and insect specimens, coins, medals, and other curiosities acquired from around the world. Upon his death in 1753, he bequeathed a whopping 71,000 items to England for £20,000, forming the foundation not only of the British Museum but the British Library and their Natural History Museum.

It does seem there can be as many types of museums as there are kinds of things to display in the world! We have archaeological museums that display ancient artefacts, ruins, and even the fossils of our human ancestors; national museums that showcase a country's cultural and political history; history museums that depict the past of a particular locale such as a building, house, or historic site; and natural history museums that display specimens from nature to teach us about the natural world such as the oceans, the earth, or the dinosaurs.

There are also science museums or science centres where you can learn about the galaxies or how electricity works, and art museums or art galleries where you can admire a sculpture or understand how watercolours first came about. There are even maritime museums that specialise in preserving and exhibiting discovered shipwrecks and war museums that specialise in presenting military objects and technology like weapons, uniforms, and war decorations.

Can you name a type of museum and check if they exist in the world? And in case you were wondering, yes, there are children's museums, bicycle museums, spectacle museums, fashion museums, toy museums, and even a museum dedicated to all things related to writing. (Can you guess what this museum is called and where it is in the world? Keep reading to find out!) Another interesting one is the Museum of Illusions, founded in Croatia in 2015, featuring magic tricks, optical illusions, and immersive experiences that play with your brain's perceptive processes.

If you become a museum curator, what type of museum would you like to work in and why? Although there is such a mind-boggling array of museums to consider, they all fulfil the following key functions: to collect, classify, display, inform one's audience, and shape the story of an exhibition's subject matter. So what important skills does a museum curator need to best fulfil these functions of a museum? Can you imagine what it would take, for example, to work as a curator at the Japan Stationery Museum in Tokyo? (Yes, this is the museum dedicated to all things writing!)

Firstly, you must know how to be organised. As a museum curator, it helps to possess keen attention to detail and be thorough and meticulous in your work. Just imagine missing the installation of that third spinal plate on the stegosaurus or mislabelling an ancient Egyptian kitchen knife as a teenage girl's bathroom comb! Museum curators need to not only know their subject matter well but certainly feature them correctly too.

As a museum curator, you could also be tasked to catalogue hundreds, perhaps even thousands, of different items while also keeping these records up to date as a collection expands. So besides having an organised mind, you will certainly need to be skilled in using computer software packages that assist in such cataloguing. We wouldn't want to misplace that one-of-a-kind 34 million-year-old Lepidoptera (butterfly) wing fossil!

Next, it helps to develop sound business management skills such as budgeting, planning, prioritising, and negotiating. This will enable you to skillfully manage and optimise a museum's budget when it comes to purchasing a collection or acquiring materials to set up an upcoming exhibition. You may also need to find the best and most cost-effective solution to store a collection. We certainly do not want that rare Qing Dynasty robe to get mouldy or moth-eaten!

It is also useful to develop good relationship-building skills to cultivate warm ongoing partnerships with a museum's various collaborators, such as donors, artists, schools, or cultural institutions. As part of a wider community, a museum contributes to the quality of life within a locale, and a museum curator supports this endeavour through their work of recreational and educational engagement with the public.

In many ways, a museum curator is like a bridge between a collection and an audience.
HISTORY
A curator will need to be able to explain to us the meaning behind a particular object, what it is for, when it was discovered and by whom, and so on. It is important for a curator to know how to put all these pieces together and clearly convey such information to visitors possibly from all walks of life and across different ages and backgrounds.

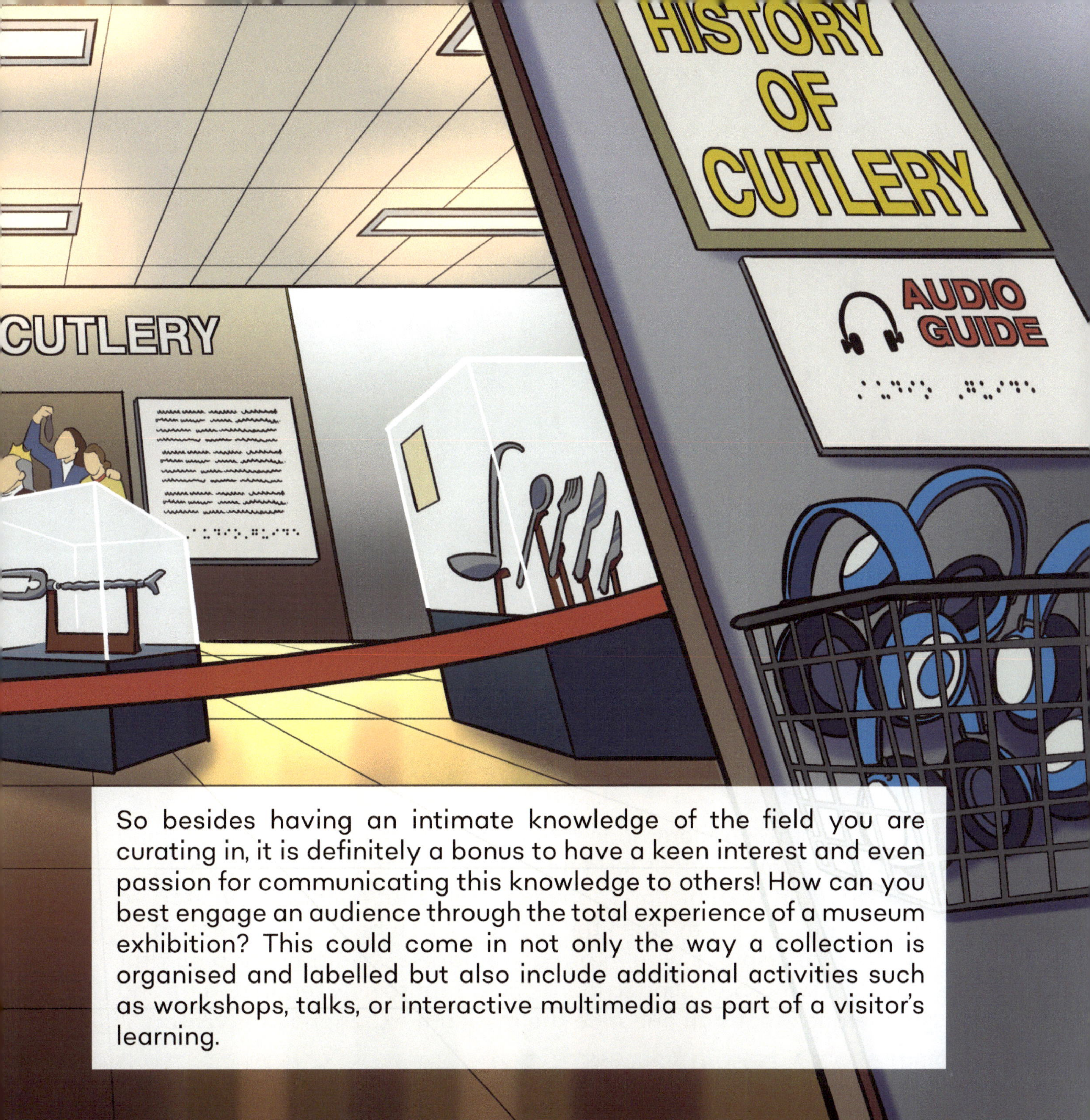

So besides having an intimate knowledge of the field you are curating in, it is definitely a bonus to have a keen interest and even passion for communicating this knowledge to others! How can you best engage an audience through the total experience of a museum exhibition? This could come in not only the way a collection is organised and labelled but also include additional activities such as workshops, talks, or interactive multimedia as part of a visitor's learning.

A good curator understands that people learn in different ways and can incorporate various learning techniques to create an immersive and engaging exhibit. Interactive exhibits that encourage visitors to touch, feel, and even smell the artefacts can be just as effective as traditional displays with informative panels. Additionally, a curator should always be willing to learn and adapt to new technologies and techniques that can enhance the museum experience for visitors.

Depending on the type, scale, and duration of an exhibition, another crucial skill of a museum curator is the ability to work well in a team. You may be liaising with a wide variety of people, such as marketing personnel needing to know more about the exhibition in order to publicise it, operational crew managing special needs access and visitor crowds, and technicians transporting and setting up the collection.

Because of this, it helps, once again, to be organised and know how to be calm when faced with pressing decisions or deadlines. You are likely needed to take on a leadership role when it comes to getting projects moving along and exhibitions successfully presented to the public.

FINAL YEAR EXIBIT

So, plenty of initiative, focus, and problem-solving skills are definite pluses! You could say a museum curator is something like a magical multitasking middleman.

So putting these skills together, a typical day in the life of a curator running up to an art exhibition, for example, may look something like this: receiving shipments of a collection, working with the office of the registrar to check that everything has arrived safely, and installing the art pieces with your team. Depending on the nature of the exhibition, you could also be working closely with the artist or donor whose work the museum is showcasing, finding the best way to shape the gallery space for visitors to encounter the artwork.

Because of the extensive knowledge usually required in the role of a museum curator, one way to begin your first steps into the world of museum curation is to undertake a degree of study with a university or institute of higher learning. This may look like an undergraduate programme in any of the following subjects: fine art or art history, archaeology or ancient history, museum or heritage studies, the natural sciences, anthropology, and national or cultural history.

Alternatively, you may decide to take on a non-museum-related area of study, such as a Bachelor of Science in Maritime Studies, and then move on to equip yourself with a postgraduate qualification in museum or gallery work. That way, you could apply your knowledge, perhaps in maritime technology, to organise an exhibition of ancient cargo ships - hopefully, without feeling too lost at sea!

If you prefer a less academic route, there is also the option of an apprenticeship programme for the aspiring professional museum curator. This is where you develop your skills through real-life experiences before getting appointed in a more permanent role with a heritage institution. In the UK alone, there are over 700 different apprenticeship categories, such as archaeological technician, archivist and records manager, and other museum supportive roles, such as marketing assistant or retail manager.

And if you're wondering what to do in your free time (besides reading about how to be a museum curator!), you could also consider getting involved as a volunteer with a local cultural institution. Volunteers act as ambassadors for the history of an area by providing free tours of heritage sites, national monuments, or museum exhibitions to members of the public. Volunteering is a fun and interactive way of learning about your local community. Who knows, with increased experience, you may get to train other new volunteer guides too!

So, would you like to be a museum curator? Do you feel inspired to explore the sometimes strange but certainly eye-opening world of rare artefacts or precious art collections? Nowadays, there are even exhibition concepts such as virtual museums entirely run online, and pop-up museums that showcase temporary exhibits, and travelling museums that tour a collection from place to place around the world!

Perhaps you may even come up with an idea for one of these museums one day. What might that museum be, and how might you showcase the collections to the public? Museum curators have the ability to not only bring the past to life but weave magnificent stories out of seemingly unknown objects to expand our minds and our understanding of how things came to be in the world around us.

My Inspiration

Shubhi Saxena
Founder, Unibino

As a parent in this ever-changing world, it can sometimes feel overwhelming when it comes to our children's futures. New technologies seem to be arising almost every day, and with so many innovations, it creates unique professions which many of us wouldn't have dreamed to be necessary only a few years ago. Which to me is a good thing. Because with so much variety, my children can have the opportunity to pick a career that will fit their personalities and build upon their strengths. As you may imagine, this desire within me to provide my children with the resources they needed to thrive, led me to search out books that would be easy enough for them to understand while teaching them about various professions.

Only, I found that these books were few and far between. Even if I could find a book about a certain profession geared towards young readers, I found them sparse inside and limited to only certain careers that may not fit my children's abilities. This is when I came up with the idea to write my own children's books, teaching them about all the various careers in the modern world. After months of researching different professions and learning more than I ever expected, I quickly realised this was going to be a bigger project than I first anticipated. I dove into the histories of these professions, discovering links to the past, and why these professions were now so important.

Ultimately my goal was to offer my children options, to show them that there is no one set path for everyone. But in this, I stumbled upon something bigger. I wanted to share this with future generations. To share with all children and parents about these careers, to help spark curiosity, and to instil a passion for the future. Everyone has special talents and abilities, and I hope that this series will be able to offer clarity and inspiration to children around the world. Because at the end of the day, it's never too early to start dreaming and never too late to take action. With this, I hope you enjoy this series and that your young ones become the best versions of themselves as they can achieve.